Karen's Plane Trip

**Look for these
and other books about Karen
in the
Baby-sitters Little Sister Series:**

Little Sister

Karen's Plane Trip
Ann M. Martin

Illustrations by Susan Tang

A
LITTLE APPLE
PAPERBACK

SCHOLASTIC INC.
New York Toronto London Auckland Sydney

This book is for
Carrie Danziger,
who is a little sister
and a big sister.

Activities by Nancy E. Krulik

ISBN 0-590-44834-X

12 11 10 9 8 7   4 5 6/9

Printed in the U.S.A.   40

First Scholastic printing, July 1991

Packing and Unpacking

I heard a humming noise outside our house. I ran to my bedroom window and looked up. A plane was flying overhead.

"Airplane!" I cried, even though no one could hear me. My little brother, Andrew, was playing at a friend's house. Mommy was downstairs. Seth was at work. (Seth is my stepfather.)

Usually, I do not get too excited about airplanes. But in just a few days, I was going to be flying on one all by myself.

I was going to fly to the state of Nebraska to visit Granny and Grandad. (They are Seth's mother and father. They live on a farm.)

"Hey, airplane!" I called out my window. "Soon I will be riding on one of you. We will zoom through the sky together!"

I turned around. I went back to my bed. I was doing something very important. I was packing for my trip. A suitcase lay open on the bed. I was not going to leave for awhile, but I wanted to be prepared.

"Goosie," I said to my stuffed cat, "I will bring you to the state of Nebraska with me. But I will not pack you yet. You would not want to be stuck in a suitcase for four days. Besides, if you are all packed up, how can I sleep with you at nighttime?"

Goosie did not answer, of course. But I talked to him anyway. I am Karen Brewer. I am seven years old. My brother is four, going on five. We both have blond hair and

2

blue eyes and some freckles. I like animals, real ones and stuffed ones. Both kinds are good for talking to. I think this is because they cannot answer back — unless you imagine that they can talk.

"Goosie," I went on, "I hope you are not nervous about flying to the state of Nebraska. . . . You aren't? Good. Neither am I. I have flown lots of times before. I have never flown *alone*, but I do not think that will matter." I put a Monopoly game on top of the things I had already piled on my suitcase. "And I've been away from home before, too. I even went to overnight camp. Of course, Kristy was there, and so were her friends." (Kristy is my big stepsister.) "But I do not think I will mind staying with Granny and Grandad by myself. . . . For two entire weeks. . . . Will I?"

I looked at my suitcase again.

"Oh, my gosh! I almost forgot my roller skates!" I added my skates to the pile. Then I added five books, my new troll doll, and

a bottle of bubble bath. I tried to close the suitcase.

I could not do it.

"Uh-oh," I said. I peered under the Monopoly game. Maybe, I thought, I do not need to bring *all* of my shirts with me. And maybe I do not need a towel and a washcloth. I bet I can borrow those things from Granny.

I took a whole lot of stuff out of the suitcase. I threw it on the floor. Ah. I could close the suitcase. But now I did not have *any* shirts. I put four back in. I took out the troll. I took out Monopoly and my roller skates. The suitcase closed, but there was not enough room for Goosie.

"Need some help, Karen?" asked Mommy. She was standing outside my room.

I shook my head. "No, thank you. I want to do this myself."

"Did you remember pajamas?" asked Mommy.

"Oops," I said.

"Socks?"

"Uh-oh."

Three days later, my suitcase was packed.

Plane Games

Before I left for the state of Nebraska, I had to say good-bye to a *lot* of people. Why? Because I have two families. Both of them live here in Stoneybrook, Connecticut. Mommy and Andrew and Seth are the people in one family. The other family is much bigger. The people in that family are Daddy; Elizabeth (she's my stepmother); Nannie (that's Elizabeth's mother); my stepbrothers Charlie, Sam, and David Michael; my stepsister Kristy; and Emily Michelle, who is my adopted sister.

The reason my mommy and daddy live in two houses is that they are divorced. First Mommy and Daddy got married. They had Andrew and me. Then they decided that they did not love each other anymore. They still loved Andrew and me, but *they* were not in love. So they got divorced. After that, they each married again. Mommy married Seth, and they live in a little house. Daddy married Elizabeth, and they live in a big house. Most of the time, Andrew and I live at the little house. But every other weekend, and also on some holidays and vacations, we live at the big house.

Usually I do not go to Daddy's on a Thursday. But on the Thursday before my plane trip, I went there for supper. After supper, it was time to say good-bye to everyone.

I started with Emily. "Bye-bye!" I said.

Emily smiled. She waved her hand. "Bye-bye!" (Emily is only two and a half.)

I hugged Emily tightly.

"Don't hug *me!*" cried David Michael. He is seven years old. "Paws off!"

"Okay, okay," I replied. " 'Bye, David Michael."

" 'Bye, Professor." ("Professor" is David Michael's nickname for me. He calls me that because I wear glasses.)

By the time I had said good-bye to everyone else, I was crying.

"Don't be sad," said Kristy. "Think about tomorrow night."

"Oh, yeah!" The next night my two best friends were coming to Mommy's house for supper. Nancy is my little-house best friend. She lives next door to Mommy. (She and Granny are pen pals!) Hannie is my big-house best friend. She lives across the street from Daddy. I was looking forward to our supper party.

"I can't believe you are leaving tomorrow," said Hannie sadly.

It was Friday night. My supper party had begun. Seth and Mommy let my friends and me eat at the picnic table in the back-yard by ourselves.

"I know," I said to Hannie. "And I will be flying all alone."

"Are you scared?" asked Nancy.

"Nah," I said. "Well . . . maybe just a teeny, *tiny* bit."

"Guess what," said Hannie. "Nancy and I have presents for you. They will keep you from being scared on the plane."

"Presents?" I exclaimed. (I just love presents.)

Nancy and Hannie ran into my house. When they came outside again, they were each carrying a book. They handed the books to me.

"These will keep you busy," said Nancy. "Look. Crossword puzzles, dot-to-dots, word searches, mazes. Tons of fun stuff!"

"Thank you!" I said.

My friends and I looked through the books. I felt happy and excited. But when Hannie and Nancy had to go home, we all cried.

10

Good-bye!

On Saturday morning I woke up early. I put on my *very best* party clothes: a blue dress with lace at the neck and all around the bottom, white tights (even though the weather was hot), and my shiny black Mary Jane shoes. Then I fixed my hair in a ponytail. I tied it with a bunch of blue ribbons. Since I wanted to look extra nice on the plane, I added some jewelry. I put on all the rings that I have gotten at the dentist's office. Then I put on five plastic bracelets and a little gold necklace. I looked in the mirror. Perfect.

As soon as breakfast was over, Mommy said to me, "All ready, honey?"

I nodded. "Yup. I have my suitcase and my fancy purse and the Fun Bag."

Seth had given me the Fun Bag. It was a tote with the words FUN BAG printed on it. Inside, Seth had put crayons, a coloring book, pencils, and a drawing pad. I had added a Bobbsey Twins mystery and the books from Hannie and Nancy. (Plus a compass in case the pilot got lost.)

"Do you have your glasses?" Mommy asked.

"All packed." I was wearing one pair of glasses. I had put my reading glasses in my pocketbook, plus my spending money, and some stamps in case I wanted to write letters or postcards.

"Time to go, then," said Seth.

It took a long time to drive to the airport. On the way, Andrew and I played I Spy and the license-plate game. Andrew won at I Spy. I won at license plates. (This may have been because I can read and Andrew cannot.) But I *was* the one who first saw the license plate from Mississippi.

"Are we almost there yet?" Andrew began to whine.

"Believe it or not, we are," answered Mommy.

We arrived at the airport an hour before my plane was supposed to leave. "What are we going to do for a whole hour?" I asked.

"You'll see," said Seth.

First we had to check my suitcase. I could not bring it on the plane with me. It was too big. But I could bring my purse and the Fun Bag.

Then Seth said, "Let's look around the airport."

I have been to this airport lots of times. But I had forgotten how much there is to see. Andrew and I watched some planes take off and land. We looked in a toy store.

We bought crackers from a vending machine.

Soon it was time to wait for *my* plane.

Mommy and Seth and Andrew and I sat in a row of plastic chairs. A flight attendant came and talked to us. "I'm Gayle," she said. "You must be Karen Brewer." (I nodded.) "I will be your stewardess today. How would you like to be the first passenger on the plane?"

"Yes!" I said. I jumped up. I followed Gayle. Mommy and Andew and Seth followed me. I really was the first passenger on the plane.

"Here is your seat," said Gayle. She showed me how to buckle my safety belt. Then she showed me how to put my things under the seat in front of me.

Gayle left my family and me alone for a few minutes.

"Well," said Seth, "I guess it's time to say good-bye."

"Okay." I said good-bye to my family. I wanted to cry. But I told myself not to.

You want to look grown-up, don't you? I thought.

Andrew cried, though. "I want to go with Karen!" he shrieked. (Mommy and Seth had to drag him off the plane.)

"Good-bye!" I called after them. "I'll call you tonight!"

Karen's Plane Trip

"Please prepare for takeoff," said a voice on the intercom.

"Still buckled up, Karen?" asked Gayle.

"Yup." I liked having my own personal stewardess.

The plane rolled down the runway. It went faster and faster. Then its nose tilted up. We were in the sky. I gazed out of my window. Below me, the ground looked crooked. And everything grew smaller and smaller and smaller. Soon the plane was very, *very* high in the sky. Clouds rolled by the windows. Now the voice on the intercom said, "You are free to move about the cabin."

I knew what that meant. We could walk around the plane. But when we were in our seats, we should buckle our belts. I got out the Fun Bag. Then I pulled down my tray. I wanted to color and maybe do a few puzzles. I also wanted to let some of the passengers know that I was seven years old — and flying *alone*. But the man next to me was reading a book. And the woman next to him had opened her briefcase. She was looking through papers, and writing things on a notepad.

I could tell that they did not want to be disturbed.

I reached above me and turned on my light. I noticed that next to the light was a big yellow button with a picture of a person on it. Just to see what would happen, I pushed the button. A tiny red light came on, and I heard a *ping*. But nothing happened . . . until Gayle leaned over the man and woman and said, "Did you call me, Karen? Are you all right?"

Oh! The button called a flight attendant.

"Um," I said, "um . . . I'm a little thirsty."

"Beverage service is about to begin," Gayle told me. "Can you wait a minute?"

"Yup." I settled back in my seat. I felt *very* grown-up.

Boy. The people on the plane sure kept me busy. Before the drink cart even started down the aisle, Gayle came back.

"Would you like to see the cockpit?" she asked me. "And meet the pilot?"

What silly questions. Of course I would.

Gayle led me to the front of the plane. She opened the door to the cockpit. I looked at the dials and switches. I said hello to the pilot *and* the co-pilot. Then the pilot gave me . . . another activity book! And he pinned a pair of flying wings to my dress.

When I returned to my seat, I was just in time to get a drink.

"Orange juice, please," I said to the flight attendant. When he handed me the cup, I handed him a quarter. For a tip, since the drink was free. But the man just smiled and said, "Thanks, but you keep that."

Then lunch was served. Another flight attendant walked along the aisle. She was pushing a cart full of trays. She handed one to me. Then she asked the man and woman next to me if they wanted lunch. But they said no and kept working.

Darn. I'd been hoping we could talk while we ate.

"How much is lunch?" I asked the stewardess. I reached for my purse.

"Oh, it's free," she said.

Goodness. If it was free, why weren't the man and the woman eating?

I ate my lunch slowly. Then I colored for awhile. Then I read for awhile. I was right in the middle of a chapter when my eyes began to close. I fell sound asleep.

Granny and Grandad

I did not wake up until Gayle touched my arm and said, "Karen. Karen? We're about to land."

"Oh, no!" I cried. "I missed the rest of the plane ride."

Gayle smiled. "Well, you're rested up and ready to meet your grandparents." She hurried down the aisle.

I glanced at the people sitting next to me. The man had put his book away. The woman had closed her briefcase.

"Hi!" I said to them. "I'm seven. I'm visiting my grandparents all by myself. I live in Connecticut."

"That's where I live," said the man.

"Hey, do you want a souvenir from our plane trip?" I asked. "Just a second." I reached under the seat. I pulled out the Fun Bag. Then I found three pictures that I had colored. I gave one to the man. I gave one to the woman, too. Even though she had not said where she lived. She did tell me that the picture was lovely, though. So I signed *both* pictures.

The plane landed with a bump. "We're in Nebraska!" I cried.

When the plane had stopped, Gayle came to my seat. "You get to be the first passenger off the plane," she told me.

She led me up the aisle. "Good-bye!" I called to the man and woman. "Good-bye!" I called to the flight attendants. We passed the cockpit. "Good-bye!" I called to the pilot and co-pilot. "I'm glad I didn't need my compass."

I held Gayle's hand tightly as we walked into the airport. The terminal was very crowded. How would we ever find Granny and Grandad? But suddenly — there they were. They ran to me. Their arms were wide open. We hugged each other. Granny cried.

"I'm so glad to see you!" she said.

Gayle talked with Granny and Grandad for a few moments. Then we said goodbye. "Oh, Gayle! Here's a picture for you." I handed her the last of the pictures I had colored. "I signed it, too."

"Thank you," said Gayle. Then she added, "Karen, I don't think I'll ever forget you."

Granny took my Fun Bag, and Grandad led the way to the place where we picked up my suitcase. He lifted it easily, and we stepped outside.

"Gosh, it's *hot*," I said.

"Welcome to Nebraska," Grandad replied.

"Do you live right around here?"

"Nope. We have a bit of a drive ahead of us. Okay, here we are."

I looked around. We were in the parking lot, standing next to a very ugly, rusty pickup truck. Part of it was painted white, part was painted green.

Grandad opened the door. He tossed my suitcase behind the seat. Then he and Granny and I climbed inside. We sat squished together. I was in the middle.

"Where's your car?" I asked. It must have broken down. My grandparents must have borrowed this truck.

"You're sitting in it," said Granny.

Yuck. I was not so sure I liked Nebraska.

But then Grandad said, "Wait until you see the farm, Karen. All the cows, some hogs, and Pearl and Sheppy. They're our cat and dog. Plus, you can ride on the tractor."

"And help in the vegetable garden," added Granny.

Well, *those* things sounded like fun.

"There's even a girl just up the road who's about your age," Grandad went on. "Her name's Tia. I think you'll like her."

Okay. Maybe Nebraska would not be so bad after all.

On the Farm

I was wrong. Nebraska was awful. Well, at least Granny and Grandad's farmhouse was. It was gigundo yucky. Maybe the farm was okay. But not the house.

We were driving along a flat road. I did not see many trees. Suddenly Grandad said, "There it is, Karen!"

"What?"

"Our farm. It's straight ahead. See the silo? And the barn?"

They were way off in the distance. But I could see them. As we drove closer to the farm, I saw other things. I saw the tractor. I saw a field of cows. I saw some gardens. I saw a pigpen and a chicken coop.

Then I saw the house. It was white. It needed to be painted. The front porch was sagging. Some shingles were missing.

This is where Seth grew up? I thought. This is where I have to stay for *two weeks?*

"Okay. Everybody out!" said Granny.

The truck had reached the end of a long driveway. Grandad had finished parking. Slowly I climbed out of the truck. I stood by Granny. "Come on inside," she said. "I'll show you your room."

Granny stepped up the rickety porch steps as if they were made of cement. I was afraid to follow her. I was afraid I would fall through the boards. Probably a snake would get me then. (But nothing happened.)

Granny and Grandad showed me to my room. It was pretty, I guess. But it was HOT. Warm air blew through the open windows. There was no air conditioner.

("Air conditioners are a waste of money," said Granny.) There was also no clock radio and no night-light.

Downstairs I looked everywhere, but I could not find a TV — or a CD player or even a record player. Just a couple of old radios.

"Where's the TV?" I asked timidly.

"TV?" Grandad repeated. "Another waste of money. Besides, we don't have cable. And the reception is rotten here."

"Does Tia have a TV?"

"Nope. Sorry, honey," said Grandad.

I did not bother to ask about the CD player or the clock radio.

But I did ask, "Are your telephones cordless?"

Granny laughed. "We've just got a regular old phone. It's been on the wall for years. It's in the kitchen."

I knew better than to say, "Just one phone?"

My stomach felt *awful*. I was surprised

Granny and Grandad had electricity. Or bathrooms.

"We've got plenty of animals," Grandad reminded me.

Yeah, I thought. Cows way out in the field. A bunch of pigs and chickens. Even Pearl was a barn cat, an outdoor cat. My only hope was Sheppy. Anyway, all the animals in the world did not make up for a stuffy bedroom without a night-light. And a quiet, rundown house. And only one phone. And especially no TV.

What did Granny and Grandad *do* at night? What did Tia do? What did they do on rainy days?

Maybe I could talk Granny and Grandad into driving to the store and buying a TV. Also a VCR. And a few movies.

Nah. If Granny thought air conditioners were a waste of money, she would never buy a VCR or movies. She would probably not even *rent* movies.

Boo.

"I Want to Come Home!"

I was hot and tired, so I took a nap before dinner.

After dinner, Grandad said, "Would you like to call home, Karen?"

"Oh, yes!" I cried. I could not wait to talk to Mommy and Seth. They would get me out of this mess somehow. Anyway, I had promised them I would call that night.

Granny dialed the phone. First she talked to Mommy and Seth. Then Grandad talked to Mommy and Seth and Andrew. Then my grandfather handed me the phone. He

30

stood there. Granny stood next to him. They smiled at me.

I smiled back . . . but I needed privacy.

"I'm just going to talk out here," I told them. I ducked into the hallway. Then I saw the coat closet. I pulled the receiver into the closet. I closed the door partway. I turned on the light. There. My very own phone booth.

"Mommy?" I said.

"Hi!" replied Mommy. "I'm right here. Seth's on, too."

"How was your plane trip?" asked Seth.

"Fine," I said quickly. "But I do not like the state of Nebraska at all. Granny and Grandad don't have a TV or a night-light or a record player or air-conditioning or *any*thing. There's nothing to do here. The animals are no fun and there are no kids to play with and probably there are snakes under the porch. Plus, I *miss* you. I want to come home!"

"Karen," said Seth gently, "you haven't really seen the farm yet, have you?"

"No," I admitted.

"Well, Granny and Grandad will take you on a tour tomorrow. You have to understand about the farm. You have to understand how Granny and Grandad like to live. Besides, you'll find plenty of things to do. You can feed the chickens, you can help Granny with her baking — "

"I do not want to do *chores*," I whined.

"Maybe you're a little bit homesick," suggested Mommy.

"Yes! That's it. I'm homesick," I agreed.

"But remember sleepaway camp? You were afraid to go to Camp Mohawk. Then, once you'd been there awhile, you had lots of fun."

"*Kristy* was there. I'm all alone here."

"Give it a chance," said Mommy. "You have to stay until tomorrow anyway. It's too late to come home now."

"Okay-ay," I sang. "But I thought I'd let you know that I did not even bring the right clothes." (This was true.) "Grandad is wearing overalls and Granny is wearing jeans. I mostly brought fancy clothes."

"We'll talk tomorrow, sweetie," said Mommy.

"All right." I said good-bye to Mommy and Seth. Then I walked back into the kitchen and handed the phone to Granny.

"Thank you," said Granny. "Okay, bedtime."

"Bedtime! It's only eight-thirty!" I exclaimed. "I'm not going to be going to school tomorrow."

"No, but we get up pretty early around here," Grandad told me.

I did not want to be rude, but I had to ask, "What are you guys going to do now?" (They could not watch TV.)

"Oh, we're going to bed, too," said Granny. "Sleep tight."

The *grown*-ups were going to bed at eight-thirty? Gosh.

Soon I climbed into the bed in my room. I kicked the covers off. The room was still HOT. I could not fall asleep. I will *never* fall asleep here, I said to myself.

When the Rooster Crows

I did fall asleep, though. I know that because later on, I heard sounds that woke me up. A rooster was crowing. Sheppy was barking. I could hear pots clanging. And I thought I smelled coffee. But how could that be? Those are morning things — and it was dark outside. I looked at my watch. It read 4:50.

Okay. Maybe Granny and Grandad get up when the rooster crows. But I don't have to . . . do I? I wondered.

I decided that maybe I better. I could not go back to sleep anyway.

So I got dressed. I almost put on the pants I had packed. But I put on another fancy dress instead. I did not want to be asked to do chores. I clickety-clacked into the kitchen, wearing my Mary Janes.

Granny and Grandpa were fixing a big breakfast. On the table were toast and fruit and bacon and juice.

"Good morning!" said Granny. Then she added, "I'm sorry, but we will have to make do without milk and eggs this morning. We ran out of a few things. But we will have them later when the milking has been done and the eggs have been collected." (Granny did not say how nice I looked.)

"Can't you just *buy* some milk and eggs?" I asked. "Go to the Seven-Eleven. That's what we do when we're out of something. They're open twenty-four hours, you know. All day and all night."

Grandad smiled. "That's a good idea, but

the nearest store is almost thirty miles away, where the nearest town is."

I did not know what to say. I could not imagine living so far from a store. I ate my breakfast quietly. Then I helped to clear the table. I even dried the dishes.

So I was surprised when I heard Granny say to me, "Honey, could you please feed the chickens this morning? I would really appreciate it."

Feed the chickens? In my party dress? And my best shoes?

"Maybe you should change your clothes," suggested Granny.

"Okay," I replied.

I stomped upstairs to my room.

I took off my dress and hung it up. I put my Mary Janes away. Then I pulled on a pair of pants, a shirt, and my sneakers.

"I have to go feed a bunch of chickens now," I told Goosie.

Goosie stared at me with his button eyes.

"I hate Nebraska," I added.

Tia

Feeding the chickens was not as bad as I had thought it would be. At least it was something to do. When I was finished, I was bored. And it was only seven o'clock. If I were in Connecticut I would still be in bed.

"Granny?" I said. I was scuffling my feet around the kitchen. I was trying to figure out what to do for the next thirteen and a half hours.

Before I could say any more, Granny interrupted me. "How about a tour of the farm, Karen?" she asked. "You have barely seen it."

"Sure," I replied. (If the tour lasted for two hours, then I would only have eleven and a half hours to kill.)

"Good," said Granny. "Grandad is in the barn. Let's go find him."

"Yikes!" I cried as soon as we were outside. "There are four strangers coming up your driveway, Granny."

"They aren't strangers," Granny told me. She waved to the people. They waved back. "They are our hired hands. They help Grandad and me to run the farm. They work here whenever they can. They're high-school students."

"Oh."

"Karen, meet Angela, Frank, Missy, and Wade."

"Hi," we said.

"See you later!" called Granny.

Granny and I walked to the barn. We were greeted by a *meow*.

"Oh, is that Pearl?" I asked.

"Yup," said Granny. "You can pick her up. She's friendly."

"Hi there, Pearl," I said. I lifted her to my face. She began to purr.

"She likes you," said Granny.

I was feeling a little better. Guess what happened next. Granny let me climb into the hayloft. I jumped around in the dusty straw.

Then Granny and Grandad showed me the pigs. I was surprised. Pigs are *furry*. And most of them are not pink.

We stood at the edge of the pasture. The cows ran over to us. I petted four of them.

Grandad showed me the crops that were growing — sugar beets, soybeans, wheat, and oats. He even took me for a ride on the tractor, and he let me steer!

We walked away from the fields. "Come see what's in this building," said Granny. "It's called the brooder house. I think you will be surprised."

Granny led me into a very warm wooden building.

"Look over here," she said. "These eggs are being allowed to hatch. Usually we collect the eggs to eat or to sell. But sometimes we need more chickens. The eggs should hatch before you go home."

"Cool!" I said. But it was hard to believe that fuzzy, fluffy yellow chicks would come out of those hard brown eggs.

"Hi!" called a voice as Granny and Grandad and I left the brooder house.

"Hello, Tia!" replied Grandad. "Karen, look who's here."

I could not believe that the person standing in front of me was a girl. Her hair was cut very short. She was wearing overalls and a white shirt. And she was holding a *boy's* bike.

I knew that Granny and Grandad wanted me to be nice. So I said hello to Tia, too. "Is that your brother's bike?" I asked her.

Tia shook her head. "Nope. I don't have any brothers. Or sisters."

So how come she rode a boy's bicycle? I decided Tia was weird.

"Well, gotta go," I said.

I could tell that it was going to be a lo-o-o-ng vacation.

The Vegetable Garden

The next morning, as soon as breakfast was over, Granny said, "Karen, do you like to garden?"

"I guess so," I replied. I had not done much gardening.

"Good," said Granny. "I'm glad you wore your pants again. I will show you my vegetable garden. I grow all our own vegetables there."

"Why? Because the Seven-Eleven is so far away?" I asked.

"No. I just enjoy keeping a garden. Come

outside with me. You can see how lettuce and beans and carrots grow."

"Okay." I followed Granny out the back door. I had learned to jump straight off the porch, away from any snakes. That way I did not have to walk down those steps. (I *never* went barefoot outdoors.)

"Here it is," Granny said a few moments later.

We had reached a leafy garden. It was not very big. But by the sign at the end of each neat row, I could see that Granny was growing lots of things. Even corn — and eggplants.

"You're growing a salad!" I exclaimed.

Granny showed me each kind of plant. Some of them were surprising. Lettuce grows right out of the ground. Carrots are root vegetables. You have to dig them up. You have to dig up potatoes and radishes, too. The eggplants and beans and tomatoes grow on bushes or vines above the ground.

"How do you know when to pull up the carrots?" I asked.

"That's a good question," said Granny. "You don't always know. Sometimes you pull one up and find that it is still very little. But I can show you how to make a good guess."

That was not the only thing Granny showed me. She showed me how to weed. She showed me how to use her gardening tools. And then she said, "Karen, would you like to be in charge of the garden while you are here?"

"*Me?*" I cried. "Really? You mean I can take care of the plants?"

"And pick vegetables, too. We can have a fresh salad every night with dinner."

"A salad right out of my garden," I said. "Cool. Okay. I will take the job."

A garden is very exciting, I thought. Granny had pulled an onion out of the ground. She had pulled a pod off a vine and shown me the peas inside. Getting vegetables out of a garden in your own backyard was much more fun than just buying them in the grocery.

46

Late that afternoon, I went back to the garden. Granny helped me to pick a basket of vegetables. "Not *too* many," she said. "Just enough for a salad for three people."

We picked a head of lettuce, an onion, some beans and tomatoes, and then I pulled up two fat carrots. In the kitchen, Granny and I washed the vegetables. Granny helped me to chop them up. We tossed them in a bowl and added salad dressing.

"You made this dressing yourself, didn't you?" I said to Granny. "This is not a bottle from a store. Will you show me how to make salad dressing?"

"Yes, tomorrow evening," Granny promised.

When Grandad came back to the farmhouse, he sat at the kitchen table. I had set the table myself. I had even picked flowers and put them in a vase.

Granny let me carry my salad to the table.

I put it in front of Grandad. He served the salad. Then he took a bite.

"I think," he said, "that this is the best salad I have ever tasted."

I was gigundo happy.

11

Rain, Rain, Go Away

Two more days went by. Each morning, I worked in the vegetable garden. Each afternoon, I made a salad for supper. In between, I played with Sheppy and Pearl. I fed the chickens. I climbed in the hayloft and read my book. I was not bored for a minute. Also, I never saw a snake. And I decided that going to bed early and getting up early was not bad after all. Anyway, a rooster is a nice alarm clock.

On Thursday morning I woke up to a new sound. Rain. I peered outside. Even in the darkness, I could tell that it was pouring.

"Boo," I said. "How will I weed the garden today? How will I play with Sheppy? What will I *do?*"

All morning I tried hard to keep busy. I read. I drew pictures. I worked in my activity books. I helped Granny bake cookies. (Grandad was working in the barn.)

Finally I could not stand it a second longer. "Are you *sure* no one around here has a TV?" I asked Granny.

"Positive. I'm sorry."

"But I'm *tired* of reading and coloring and baking," I whined.

Granny looked thoughtful. "Would you like to learn how to knit?" she asked.

"Really?" I replied. I had been *dying* to learn how to knit. Back in Stoneybrook, I watched Nannie knit all the time. "Don't you think I'm too young?" I asked.

"Nonsense. I learned to knit when I was six," Granny told me.

"Okay, then. I am ready."

Granny sat next to me in the living room. She opened a bag. The bag was full of knitting needles and balls of yarn. Granny showed me how to hold two needles. She showed me how to loop the yarn around them. Soon she said, "Now you know how to do the knit stitch. That is one of the most important stitches. I think you are ready to make a headband."

"Already?" I said.

In a very short time I had knitted *two* headbands. One was red. The other was blue. (Granny worked on a sweater.)

I looked at my headbands. I thought for a moment. I bet, I said to myself, that if I can knit a headband, I can knit a scarf. I kept my thought a secret, though.

Ding-dong!

Goody. Just when I was almost bored again, the doorbell rang.

I ran to see who had come over.

On the front porch stood Tia. Rain was streaming down her poncho.

The Invention Sisters

"Hi, Tia! Come on in!" I cried.

Tia looked surprised. I could not blame her. I had not been very nice when I had met her. And I had not invited her to come over to play.

Now I was glad to see her. Granny and Grandad and Sheppy and Pearl were wonderful. But I missed playing with someone my own age. I decided that I did not mind if Tia looked like a boy.

Tia stepped inside. She took off her poncho. I hung it in the bathroom. (If it dripped into the tub, it would not make a mess.) On my way out of the bathroom, I grabbed a towel. I handed it to Tia.

"Here," I said. "You need to dry off."

When Tia was dry, I offered her some cookies. "Granny and I baked them this morning," I said. "They are quite fresh. I can make salad dressing, too. By the way, what do you do when you get bored on rainy days? Granny said you don't have a TV."

Tia shook her head. "Nope."

We were sitting at the table in the kitchen. Granny had said hello to Tia, but she was still in the living room. She was working on the sweater.

"I never watch TV," Tia told me. "I do other things."

"Today," I said, "I have already baked, read, colored, worked in my activity books, and learned how to knit." I looked at the clock. "And it is only eleven-thirty."

Tia grinned. "You know what I do? I make board games."

"You *make* board games? Like Candy Land?"

"Yup. Only I invent games about anything I want."

"Neat! I love to make things. Hey, you know what, Tia? We could invent games this afternoon. We could call ourselves the Invention Sisters."

"Yeah!" agreed Tia.

"What do we need to make a game?" I asked.

"Oak tag or cardboard, paper, Magic Markers . . . let's see. Buttons, scissors, a thumbtack, maybe glue. If you don't have buttons, it's okay."

But Granny had a whole box of buttons. She found everything else we needed, too. Soon Tia and I were sitting on the floor in my room.

"First you make a spinner," said Tia. She cut an arrow out of the oak tag. Then she

cut a circle out of the oak tag. This is what
she drew on the circle:

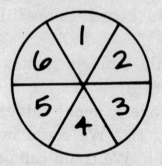

She used the thumbtack to fasten the arrow to the circle.

"See? You spin the arrow. You see what
number it stops at. If it stops at four, then
you move four spaces. Get it?"

"Yeah!"

After that, Tia and I drew a long wiggly
path on another piece of oak tag. We di-
vided the path into spaces:

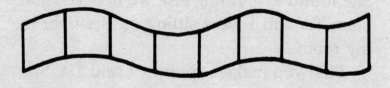

We decided to call our game On the Farm. In each space, we wrote a message like this: "Your tractor breaks down. Move back two spaces." Or, "Your chicks hatch! Move ahead three spaces."

"Okay," said Tia. "Good. Now, the first player to cross the finish line is the winner. You go first, Karen. Spin the spinner. Use a button for your playing piece."

"Thanks," I replied. "Hey, the Invention Sisters are pretty good, aren't they?"

Tia grinned. "They're the best."

13

A New Friend

That afternoon, Tia and I made two more games. They were called Going to School and The Plane Trip. They were both gigundo cool.

Guess what Tia was wearing. Her blue-jean overalls again. This time she wore them over a striped shirt. She still looked like a boy. I decided that was okay.

I also decided I would not mind having my own overalls. Grandad wore overalls every day. And Granny wore jeans every day. I had jeans, but I left them in Stoneybrook. And I did not have any overalls. It would be fun to dress like Tia. Anyway, the Invention Sisters should look more alike. Right now, we did not look like sisters. We did not even look related.

It was funny. In Stoneybrook, hardly anyone wears overalls. Except babies and little kids. But almost everyone around the farm wore them: Grandad, Tia, the hired hands. I was tired of being the only one wearing dresses or good pants.

When Tia went home that day, I asked Granny two questions. The first one was, "Can Tia and I have a sleepover on Saturday night?" The second was, "Can I buy some overalls? And maybe a hat? I need them for working in the garden."

Granny said yes to the sleepover. She said she would have to talk to Grandad about the overalls and the hat. We would have to drive all the way to town to buy them.

I hoped the answer would be yes. I *really* wanted overalls and a hat. Maybe I would even get my hair cut like Tia's. But I decided not to. I remembered the last time I had gotten a haircut. It had been a disaster.

When Granny told Grandad that I wanted to go to town, this is what Grandad said: "I think that's a fine idea. I need to pick up a few things anyway."

"Let's go tomorrow, then," Granny said.

"Yippee-e-e-e!" I cried.

Even though Friday was a different kind of day, we still had to get up early. The animals needed to be fed. This takes a long time.

When all the animals and all the people had eaten, Granny and Grandad and I piled into the pickup truck. The drive to town was so long that I fell asleep. I woke up when I heard Granny say, "Here's the town, Karen."

"Where?" I asked. I rubbed my eyes. We were driving down a dusty road.

"Right here. There's the store and there's

the bank and there's the diner. Oh, and there's the gas station," said Grandad.

This was it? The whole town?

"Stoneybrook is a little bigger, isn't it?" asked Granny.

"Yup," I said. I was thinking, Where's the ice-cream parlor? Where's the video rental? Where's the toy store? What do people do without a pet shop?

But I was surprised by the store. It looked small from the outside, but inside was — everything! You could buy clothes, food, toys, hardware, medicine, sewing stuff, school supplies, stamps, and more.

"Hi, Greta," Granny greeted a woman in the store. (Grandad had gone to the hardware department.) "This is my granddaughter. This is Karen. She's seven."

"Karen! Nice to meet you." Greta gave me a FREE lollipop. Then she helped Granny and me to pick out a pair of overalls and a straw hat. I bought them all by myself with my own money.

When we were finished in the store, Grandad said, "How about lunch, Karen?"

"In the restaurant? Sure."

We walked to the little coffee shop. I was wearing my new clothes. Granny and Grandad seemed to know *every*one in the restaurant. They introduced me to the waitresses and the customers. When anyone asked me where I came from, I said, "Well, I was born in Connecticut, but right now I live in the state of Nebraska."

Popcorn and Potatoes

At five o'clock on Saturday afternoon, the doorbell rang. I had just come in from the garden. I had been working hard. I was gigundo glad I had bought the overalls and the hat. When you work on a farm, you need those things badly.

I raced for the front door. There stood Tia. She was wearing a backpack. Her bicycle was parked by the porch.

"Ready for the sleepover?" I asked her.

"Ready!"

Tia and I had a lot to do. First we went

back to the garden. I let Tia carry the basket. We picked vegetables for another salad. (We did not need help. We could do that by ourselves.)

We were on our way back to the house when Granny called, "Karen! Tia! Would you pick six ears of corn, please?"

So we did. Then we ate dinner outside at a picnic table: salad, corn on the cob, and chicken. After dinner, Granny said, "How would you girls like to make popcorn?"

"Yes!" we cried. Granny brought out a jar of corn kernels. They were not plain old yellow kernels. They were lots of different colors — red and green and blue. When they had popped, they looked like a fluffy cloud and a rainbow all mixed together.

"Cool," I said.

"Yeah, cool," agreed Tia.

We took the popcorn upstairs. We ate it while we made another board game. This one was called Going to Hollywood.

"You know what?" I said to Tia after she had won the game.

"What?" asked Tia.

"I am making a surprise for Granny. It's because she has been so nice. Because she taught me how to garden and knit."

"What are you making?"

"I'm knitting her a whole long scarf. Pink and purple stripes. When it is finished, I am going to wrap it up. I think I will even make the wrapping paper."

"Do you know how to make potato-print paper?" asked Tia. I told her I did not. "Then I can show you," she said.

Tia and I went to the kitchen. We found a potato. Tia asked Granny to cut it in half. "This is for a secret," I told Granny. Granny left the kitchen.

Tia found a fork. She used it to press a crisscross design in one potato half. Then she made polka dots in the other potato. She used the end of a crayon for that.

"There," said Tia. "Now, all you do is pour some paint into a saucer. Then you dip the potato design in the paint — very lightly — and you stamp it all over a piece of paper. You can use white paper or colored paper."

"Tia," I said. "I wish you lived in Connecticut. Then we could always be friends."

"I wish you lived in Nebraska," Tia replied.

"Maybe we can be pen pals," I suggested.

"Maybe you could visit your grandparents every year."

"Maybe you could come to Connecticut sometime."

"Girls?" called Grandad. "Karen? Tia? It's bedtime."

"Boo," I said.

But then Grandad came into the kitchen. He said, "It's extra hot tonight. How would you like to sleep on the porch? The porch will be much cooler than the bedroom."

Sleep on the porch? Right over the snakes?

"What would we sleep in?" I asked.

"Hammocks," replied Grandad.

Wow! I looked at Tia. She was grinning. "Okay!" I said to Grandad. "Thank you!"

That night, Tia and I fell asleep in the hammocks. Above us, the stars shone. And all around us, a soft breeze blew.

Karen in Business

"Vegetables! Vegetables for sale! Get them right here! We've got carrots and peas and corn and tomatoes, eggplants, cabbages, beans, and potatoes!"

I woke up from a wonderful dream. I was so excited that I forgot where I was sleeping. I nearly fell out of the hammock.

"Tia!" I cried. And then I realized that the sun was rising. We had slept right through the rooster alarm clock. "Tia, wake up! It's late. And guess what. I have a terrific idea. We can start a business. I had a dream about it. We can sell vegetables from the garden. We'll set up a stand at the end of the drive."

"Yeah . . ." said Tia sleepily. "I have to check with my parents, though."

Tia's parents said she could stay over until five o'clock. Then Granny said we could sell some vegetables. "Just don't pick too many."

"Why not?" I asked.

Granny looked at Grandad. Grandad shrugged. Then he said, "Well, it's Sunday, Karen. There might not be much traffic today."

"Anyway, a lot of people have their own g — " Tia started to say.

But Granny interrupted her. "Run along and pick some vegetables. Why don't you start with one basketful."

"I will carry a table and two chairs outside for you," added Grandad.

"Oh, and we better make a sign!" I cried.

* * *

Later that morning, Tia and I were in business. We were sitting on chairs at the end of the driveway. In front of us was the table. We had put the vegetables on the table. We set them out in a gigundo pretty pattern. Next to the table stood our sign. It said: K-T VEGETABLES. GET YOUR FRESH VEGETABLES HERE! (K-T stood for "Karen and Tia.")

We sat outside for an hour. Two cars drove by. They did not stop.

I looked at my watch. "This is boring. I wonder what's wrong," I said.

"Maybe — " began Tia.

But suddenly I exclaimed, "Oh! I know! We did not advertise enough. No one knows about our business unless they drive by our house."

"What should we do?"

"We could make more signs," I suggested. "We could put them up and down the road. They would say things like, 'One more mile to K-T Vegetables,' and 'Just half

K-I VEGETABLES

GET YOUR FRESH
/EGETABLES HERE!

TOMATOES   RADISHES   ONIONS
CARROTS   BEANS   SQUASH
CUCUMBERS   LETTUCE   COEN

a mile to K-T Vegetables.' Everyone would want to stop and buy."

"It will take a long time to put up all those signs," said Tia.

"I know it. Hey! Look!"

A car had stopped. A woman got out. She bought four ears of corn.

"Tia! We earned a dollar!" I cried.

At four-thirty, Tia said, "I have to be home in half an hour. I better go."

"Oh." I groaned. I was very tired. Even though Tia and I had only sold two heads of lettuce, those ears of corn, and a bunch of beans. We had earned $2.59.

"How will we split that in half?" asked Tia.

"I get . . . let's see. I get one dollar and thirty cents, and you get one dollar and twenty-nine cents," I said. "The extra penny is mine because the vegetables came from my garden."

"Okay," agreed Tia.

Tia and I took the leftover vegetables back

to Granny. We carried the chairs and the table to the house.

"You know what?" I said as Tia climbed onto her bicycle. "K-T Vegetables did not make much money. But it was fun, wasn't it?"

"Gigundo fun," said Tia. Then she added, "Partner!"

New Babies

"Guess what, honey," said Grandad at breakfast one morning.

"What?"

Grandad sounded excited, but I felt sad. It was Wednesday. In three days I would have to go home. I would have to leave the farm. Boo.

"The chicks are about to hatch," Grandad told me.

"Really?" I cried. "Really, really, *really?*"

"Really," replied Grandad.

"I have never seen anything hatch. I have

never seen anything be born. Well, maybe on TV. But that doesn't count. Can I invite Tia over?"

"Of course," said Granny. "But remember that Tia has grown up on a farm. She has seen chicks hatch. And she has watched kittens and puppies and calves being born."

I called Tia anyway. She said she wanted to come over.

"See you this afternoon," she said.

"This after*noon!* But the chicks might have hatched by then."

"No, they won't," said Tia. But she came over before lunchtime.

Well, those chickies certainly took their time. Tia and I watched them for hours and nothing happened. Sitting around in the brooder house was boring. And hot.

"What's keeping them?" I asked Tia.

"They're not ready yet," she answered. "They have to be ready."

A little while later, Granny and Grandad joined us. We waited some more.

"Look at that," whispered Grandad. "It's starting."

I stared at the eggs. I saw that one was moving. A chick was poking its way out. It looked like it was working hard.

"Ooh," I said softly. Then, "Gross! What's wrong with it?"

A scrawny, dark, wet thing was struggling out of the egg. And it was not the only one. Some other eggs were hatching. And all the chicks were scrawny and dark and wet. And ugly.

"That's how chicks look when they're born," said Granny.

"I thought they would be fluffy and yellow and cute."

"They will be soon. First they have to dry off. The inside of an egg is wet. The fluid helps the chick grow and develop. You watch the chicks, now."

I watched. When the chicks were dry, they looked just right.

"Fluffy!" I said. "And cute. . . . Grandad?"

"Yes?"

"Could one of the chicks be mine, please?"

"Yours? I don't know. Well, I suppose so. It would have to live here on the farm, though."

"It would?"

"Honey, you can't take a chick on an airplane. Besides, chicks are happier living on farms with other chicks."

"Oh." I had thought a chick might make a good pet for Andrew.

Granny saw that I was disappointed. "There's one other thing," she said. "Remember that chicks grow up."

Oh, yeah. I decided that a *chicken* would *not* make a very good pet.

I smiled at Granny and Grandad. "Thank you," I said. "I would really like to have a chick of my own. And I would like it to grow up in Nebraska."

"Which chick would you like?" asked Grandad.

"That one." I pointed to the fluffiest chick of all.

"It's yours," said Granny.

My very own chick! "I will name it Tia," I announced.

"I Don't Want to Come Home!"

The rooster was crowing. Do you want to know a secret? Crowing does not sound a thing like "cock-a-doodle-doo." I do not know *who* decided that. Crowing sounds more like "er er-er er-er."

I rolled over on my tummy. "Boo," I said out loud. "Boo, boo, boo."

It was Friday. The next day would be Saturday, and I would go home. I would have to say good-bye to the state of Nebraska.

I got out of bed. I put on my overalls. I

carried my straw hat downstairs and into the kitchen.

"Good morning," said Granny and Grandad.

" 'Morning," I replied. "Do I really have to go home tomorrow?"

"I'm afraid so," said Granny.

"Then I am going to be very busy today."

"What are you going to do?"

"Last things. I have to do everything one last time. I have to play in the hayloft, and invite Tia over, and we have to invent another game. I have to say good-bye to all the animals. And, Grandad, can you give me one last ride on the tractor? And can you show me the fields one last time?"

"Certainly. If you will make me one last salad."

"Certainly."

Grandad did his morning chores. I fed the chickens. Granny made a cherry pie. She said it was for dessert that night.

When we were finished, we took a tour

of the farm. Just like we did when I first came to Nebraska. Only this time, *I* took *Granny* and *Grandad* on the tour.

"Here are the pigs," I said. "And here are the cows. This is the barn. This is the hayloft." (I stopped to play.)

Granny and Grandad pretended they had not been to a farm before.

After lunch, Tia came over.

"Here we are. The Invention Sisters!" I cried. "What shall we invent today?"

"A game called Save Our Planet," replied Tia.

"Oh, that's good. It will be about saving energy and not littering."

Tia and I worked very hard on Save Our Planet. Then we played it three times. Tia won once. I won twice.

"Let's go see the chicks," I suggested.

So the Invention Sisters ran to the brooder house. On the way, Tia asked, "How is Tia doing?" (She meant Tia the chick.)

"She's fine," I said.

"How can you tell her apart from all the others?"

"You'll see!"

In the brooder house, Tia and I stood in front of the new chicks. "Find Tia," I said to Tia.

Tia looked and looked. She began to giggle. "There she is!"

"Yup!" I had painted a tiny red dot on each of Tia's claws.

"I hope the paint is waterproof," said Tia. Then she checked her watch. "Oh, no, Karen. I have to go home now."

"Are you sure?"

"Yes."

Tia climbed onto her bicycle. We started to cry. "Good-bye!" we called. "I'll miss you!"

And I added, "Invention Sisters forever!"

Then I turned and ran inside. I telephoned Mommy. I was still crying. "I don't want to come home!" I wailed. But of course Mommy said I had to.

Karen's Gifts

"Oof." I was lugging another basket of vegetables into the house. It was time for me to make my last salad.

I decided the salad should look fancy. So Granny showed me how to make carrot curls. She showed me a special tool that makes radishes look like flowers. Then she helped me slice up an egg and a tomato. I arranged the carrot curls, the radish flowers, the egg slices, and the tomato slices in a pattern. They looked like a swirl on top of the salad.

"This is the prettiest salad I have ever seen," said Grandad as we were starting dinner.

"Thank you," I replied. I took a bite. I chewed it carefully. I swallowed. "You know what's funny?" I said.

"What?" asked Granny and Grandad.

"When I first came here, I wanted to go home. Now that it is time to go home, I wish I could stay."

Grandad smiled. "You were very grown-up to stay when you were so scared."

"I feel like I have grown up. Like maybe I am ten or eleven." I thought for a moment. "What would you have done if I had really, *really*, REALLY wanted to leave?"

"We would have let you go home," Grandad answered.

"But we would have missed you," added Granny.

I nodded. "Well, I am glad I stayed. I like the state of Nebraska."

* * *

After dinner, Granny and Grandad and I sat in the living room.

"Guess what. I have presents for you," I announced. (Granny and Grandad looked surprised.) "They are in my room," I went on. "I'll go get them." I ran upstairs. I pulled two things out from under my bed. I brought them back to the living room. "This one is for you," I said to Granny.

Granny took the package from me. "Karen, did you make the wrapping paper?"

"Yes," I said proudly. "I potato-printed it. Tia showed me how. I made the present, too."

Granny opened the box. Inside was the pink-and-purple scarf. I had finished it just in time.

"Honey, it's lovely!" Granny gave me a big hug. "Thank you."

"You're welcome. And thank you for teaching me how to knit. And garden. And bake. And make salads."

"Where's my present?" asked Grandad.

I giggled. "Right here." I gave him a very flat package. It was also wrapped in potato-print paper.

Grandad opened the package. He pulled out a piece of paper. " 'The Farm,' " he read. " 'A poem by Karen Brewer.' " He stopped to adjust his glasses. Then he went on, " 'My Granny and Grandad live on a farm. They're as nice as they can be. They work hard and take care of their animals, which is very important, you see.' "

The poem was quite long. I had written seven stanzas after that first one. The poem told about Grandad, Granny, and their farm. When Grandad finished reading it, his eyes looked a little wet. "This is one of the nicest presents I have ever been given," he said. Grandad gave me a hug.

Later, I was getting ready for bed when I thought of something. I had not given Tia my address. She needed my address if we were going to be pen pals. So I telephoned her. I told her my address, and she told me hers. Then we said good-bye again. We hung up.

"Granny? Grandad?" I said. They were tucking me in bed for my last night on the farm. "Can I come visit you again?"

"You better," said Grandad. "We need someone to feed the chickens."

"Oh, don't pay attention to him," said Granny. "Of course we want you to visit again. We will miss you when you leave."

"I'll miss you, too," I said.

The Champion Flier
of the World

The truck rattled into the parking lot at the airport.

"Here we are," said Granny.

"Boo," I replied.

"Are you scared about flying alone?" asked Grandad.

"No," I said. "Not at all. I am a champion flier now. The champion flier of the world. I just do not want to say good-bye. That's all."

But of course we had to say good-bye. Granny and Grandad walked me onto the

90

plane. I had a new personal stewardess. Her name was Joan.

"Karen," said Joan, "this is your tray, and here is your reading light — "

"I know," I said. "I know all about flying." I buckled my seat belt.

Joan smiled. "I guess you do."

"Joan? I need to tell you something," I said. Joan leaned over. I whispered, "I need to say good-bye to my grandparents. In private."

"Oh. I'll leave you alone then," Joan whispered back. She tiptoed away.

I looked at Granny and Grandad. "I guess this is it," I said. "Thank you very much for everything. Thank you for driving me to town, and for letting me play with Pearl and Sheppy, and for giving me a chick."

I was trying to be brave, but I could not help it: I began to cry.

Granny gave me a hug. "It's hard to say good-bye, isn't it?"

"Yes. It's gigundo hard."

In the end, we did not say good-bye. We hugged. I said thank you again. Then Granny and Grandad left the plane.

By the time I was finished crying, other people were finding their seats on the plane. A man sat next to me. He looked sort of like Daddy. He did not open a book. He did not open his briefcase. So I said, "Hi. I am Karen. I'm seven. I am flying alone. This is not the first time. Are you busy?"

"No," said the man. "My name is Lewis. I'm glad to meet you, Karen."

"I have my own personal stewardess. Her name is Joan. If I press that yellow button up there, Joan will come. Maybe she will get us Cokes or something."

"Thank you. That's a nice offer," replied Lewis. "But I think I'll wait until after the plane has taken off."

"Oh. Then I will, too," I said. (I did not want to be rude.) I reached under the seat for the Fun Bag. "Here is all my stuff. We could play games. Or we could just talk. Where are you going? I'm going home. I live in Connecticut. I have been visiting my grandparents. They live on a farm."

"I'm going home, too," Lewis said. "I cannot wait to see my family again."

"Do you have a big family?" I asked. "Because I do. I have parents and stepparents and a brother and stepbrothers and a stepsister and even an adopted sister. I have four grandmothers and . . ."

The plane took off. Lewis and I talked and talked. Joan came by. She asked if I would like to go to the cockpit. I could visit the pilot and the co-pilot, she said. I thought about my compass. I almost said yes. Instead I said, "No, thank you. I will stay here and talk to Lewis. There's a lot I haven't told him yet."

So Lewis and I talked. Then we played Tic-Tac-Toe and Battleships and Hangman. After that, Joan and the other flight attendants served lunch.

"Do you like this lunch?" I asked Lewis.

"Do you?" he said.

"Not really."

"Neither do I."

Lewis and I smiled at each other. Then we talked some more.

Welcome Home, Karen!

I did not fall asleep on the plane. I had to entertain Lewis. If I did not do that, he would have been very bored.

We were both working in my activity books when the plane began to land. (I was finishing a maze. Lewis was filling in a crossword puzzle.) "We are almost home!" I exclaimed. "Mommy and Seth and Andrew are going to meet me at the airport."

Whoosh. The plane was on the ground. It was racing along the runway. When it stopped, I took the Fun Bag and my purse from under the seat.

Joan came by. "Ready to meet your family?" she asked.

I said, "Yes. Can Lewis come with us?"

"Of course," replied Joan.

Joan and Lewis and I walked off the plane. (I tried to run, but Joan told me to slow down, please.)

Guess who were the very first people I saw in the airport. Mommy and Andrew and Seth! Lewis walked right up to them. He said, "You must be Mr. and Mrs. Engle. And this must be Andrew."

My little-house family looked quite surprised. "Yes . . ." said Mommy.

"Karen told me all about you. Well, have a good trip back to Stoneybrook. Nice meeting you, Karen!" Lewis walked off.

I grinned. "I'm home!" I threw my arms around Mommy and Seth. I even hugged Andrew. Then I said, "Don't worry, Mommy. I usually don't talk to strangers.

But I didn't think I could sit next to Lewis all that time and *not* talk to him. How are you guys?"

"Karen!" exclaimed Mommy. She was laughing. "How was the farm? How are Granny and Grandad? What have you been doing for the last two weeks? We missed you."

"How is your homesickness?" Andrew wanted to know.

"It's all gone! I liked the farm. I liked the state of Nebraska. Oh, by the way, I made a new friend. Her name is Tia. I have a chick named Tia, too. I watched her hatch out of an egg."

We had walked to the baggage claim. We were waiting for my suitcase.

"You have a chick?" said Andrew. "Where? Can I see it?"

I shook my head. "She's on the farm. She needs to grow up with her brothers and sisters. . . . Hey, there's my suitcase!"

Mommy picked up my suitcase. We walked outside to our car.

"How come you're wearing overalls?" asked Andrew.

"Oh, *every*one I met wore overalls. I have a straw hat, too. It's smushed into my suitcase. Hey, Andrew, Tia taught me how to *make board* games. Now we won't have to buy them anymore. We made lots. We made On the Farm and Going to Hollywood and Going to School and Save Our Planet."

Seth had unlocked the car. We climbed inside. We buckled our seat belts. We began to drive home.

"So what did you do while I was gone?" I asked Andrew.

"Mmm. Played with my trucks. Went swimming. Did you meet Pearl?"

"Yes. And Sheppy. I rode on a tractor and I played in the hayloft. Granny let me take care of her vegetable garden. And she taught me how to make salads. I bet we could grow a vegetable garden. . . . Hey, you know what, Mommy? You know what, Seth? This morning I did not want to leave

100

Nebraska. But now I am glad to be home."

"It's good to have you home, honey," said Seth.

"Thank you. Andrew, when you are older maybe you can come to Nebraska with me."

"I would like that," said Andrew.

Soon we were driving through Stoneybrook. Then we were driving down our street. And finally, there was the little house.

"Hello, little house," I said. "I'm home again."

Fun With Karen Activity Pages!

Are you going on a long trip like Karen? Or are you stuck inside on a rainy day with nothing to do? These fun activities and puzzles will keep you busy, whether you're far away or close to home!

All Packed and Ready to Go!

If you're getting ready to take a trip, here's a list of things you won't want to leave behind! Check off each one as you pack it.

- ☐ toothbrush
- ☐ toothpaste
- ☐ hairbrush
- ☐ stamps
- ☐ stationery
- ☐ pens
- ☐ camera
- ☐ film
- ☐ sunglasses
- ☐ a spare pair of glasses (if you're like Karen and you need glasses to see)
- ☐ shampoo
- ☐ books to read
- ☐ stuffed animal
- ☐ easy-to-carry games to play on the plane

Packing Play!

Here's a fun packing game you can play with your friends. It's called I Packed My Grandmother's Trunk. You will need at least one other player for the game. Here's how you play:

1. This is an alphabet game. The first player starts by saying, "I packed my grandmother's trunk. I packed an _____." The first player must say the name of an object that begins with the letter *A*. Let's suppose the first player packed an *apple*.

2. Now it is the second player's turn. He or she says, "I packed my grandmother's trunk. I packed an apple and a ball" (or anything else that begins with the letter *B*).

3. Continue taking turns, listing all the objects that came before and adding an object that begins with the next letter in the alphabet. Any player who forgets an object or says one that begins with the wrong letter is out. The last player left in the game wins!

4. For a gigundo-tough twist on this game, start with the letter *Z* and work your way backwards!

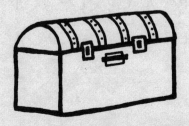

Gigundo-Fun Puzzles to Try

Karen is always looking for something to do! She has a tough time just sitting still. It's not always easy to find fun things to do on an airplane. If you're like Karen, these puzzles will keep you super busy on your trip!

Pals Forever Wordsearch!

Hannie, Nancy, and Karen are the Three Musketeers. They do everything together! Karen is sad to leave her best pals behind. How many times can you find the word PAL in this wordsearch? Look up, down, sideways, backwards, and diagonally.

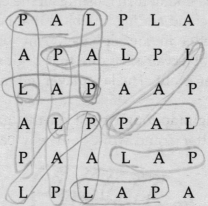

Karen Two-Two's Count by Twos Puzzle

Count by twos to connect the dots. You will see how Karen will get to the airport. Then color the picture with crayons.

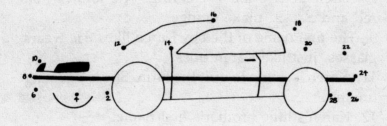

Karen's Crossword Puzzle

How much do you know about Karen? Use the clues below to fill in the puzzle on page 109.

ACROSS

2. Karen's hometown

6. Karen can be impatient. She doesn't want to wait for anything. She wants everything _____!

7. Karen does a lot of coloring. She knows that red and _____ make orange.

9. The first name of the boy Karen likes. He wears glasses, just like Karen does.

11. Karen is going to visit the farm. She is traveling on an _____.

12. Karen's little brother's first name.

DOWN

1. Karen's favorite stuffed animals are named Moosie and _____.

3. Because her parents are divorced, Karen calls herself Karen _____-_____.

4. The Three Musketeers are Karen, Hannie, and _____.

5. Karen's older stepsister and founder of The Baby-sitters Club.

8. When Karen is inside she uses her indoor voice. Where is she when she uses her outdoor voice?

10. The woman Karen is going to visit on this vacation.

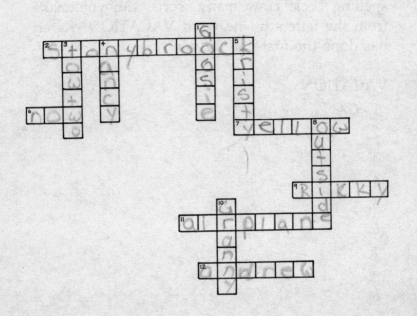

Spellbound!

Karen is a terrific speller. She's even won four spelling bees! How many words can you make from the letters in the word VACATION? Karen has done the first one for you.

VACATION
1. CAN
2.
3.
4.
5.
6.
7.
8.
9.
10.

Something's Different!

These two airport pictures are not the same. Circle the things that are different.

Up, Up, and Away!

Karen's Granny lives far away. Karen needs to take an airplane to visit her. This picture is all mixed up. Copy what you see into the matching boxes to make a picture of the airplane Karen will take.

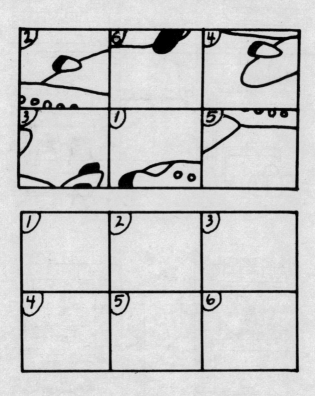

Life on a Farm

At first, Karen can only imagine what life on Granny's farm will be like. How about you? Fill in the parts that are missing.

The Amazing Alphabet Game

Even though Karen would never ever admit it, she's a little nervous about going on an airplane all by herself. So to keep herself busy she teaches Andrew to play the Alphabet Game. You can play, too. Here's how.

For every letter of the alphabet, you have to think of a girl's name, a boy's name, a place, and a thing. You use them to fill in the blanks of a poem. The poem for the letter *A* goes like this:

A, my name is *Anna* and my husband's name is *Alex*. We come from *Alabama*, and we sell *apples*.

Now it is the next player's turn.

B, my name is *Barbara* and my husband's name is *Bill*. We come from *Buffalo* and we sell *books*.

Each player takes a letter of the alphabet in turn. Any player who can't think of a word to fill in a blank is out. The last player left is the winner.

Beware! This game gets tough with letters like *Q* and *X*. Here are some fill-ins you can try!

Q:
Queenie (girl's name)
Quincy (boy's name)
Queens (a place in New York City)
Quills (a kind of pen made from a feather)

X:
Xanthe (girl's name)
Xavier (boy's name)
Xochimilco (a place near a lake in Mexico)
Xylophone (an instrument)

The License Plate Look-Out Game!

The next time your family takes a long drive, you and your brothers and sisters can keep yourselves busy with this crazy car game. All you need to play is a piece of paper and a pencil for each player.

Here's how you play:
1. Set a 30-minute time limit. Have Mom or Dad keep the time.
2. Now start looking out the window. Check out the license plates on the cars that pass by. Write down the different states listed on the license plates. Write down each state only once.
3. At the end of the 30 minutes, the player with the most states listed wins!
4. If you're playing by yourself, set lots of shorter time limits. See how many states you can find each time.

Fun Facts About the United States!

Amaze your friends with these fun facts about some of our states.

1. Did you know that Arkansas is the only state to pass a resolution on how to pronounce its name? The correct way to say Arkansas is *Ark-an-saw*.

2. Did you know that California's bristlecone pines are the oldest living things on earth? They are believed to be 4,600 years old!

3. Did you know that Karen's home state of Connecticut is the leading maker of helicopters?

4. Did you know that the first Coca-Cola was served in an Atlanta, Georgia, drugstore in 1887?

5. Did you know that Michigan is the only one of the fifty states to be touched by four of the five Great Lakes? They are: Lake Michigan, Lake Huron, Lake Erie, and Lake Superior. It is not touched by Lake Ontario.

6. Did you know the first ice cream cone was served in St. Louis, Missouri, in 1904?

7. Did you know that Rhode Island is the smallest state in the country? It covers only 1,212 square miles.

Find Your Plane Airport Maze

Most airports are huge! It can be hard to find the gate that your plane is leaving from. Help Karen get to her plane on time.

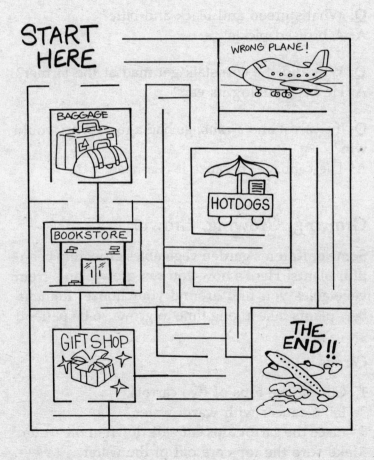

Silly Salad Jokes!

These silly fruit and vegetable jokes make Tia and Karen laugh. They're guaranteed to give you the giggles, too!

Q: What's green and black and blue?
A: A bruised pickle!

Q: Why did the cornstalk get mad at the farmer?
A: He kept pulling its ears!

Q: If a carrot and a cabbage had a race, who would win?
A: The cabbage, because it is a-head!

Growing, Growing, Grown!

Some of Karen's garden vegetables grow into beautiful plants. Here's how you can grow plants from vegetables you find around your house. Remember, plants take a long time to grow, so be patient!

Carrots

1. Cut off the tops of two carrots.
2. Fill a saucer with warm water.
3. Place the carrot tops cut-side down in the water. Make sure the tops are out of the water.

4. Put the bowl on a windowsill where it will get sunlight.

5. When the leaves start to grow and the roots sprout, plant the carrots in a flowerpot.

Dry Lima Beans

1. Fill a glass three quarters of the way to the top with warm water.

2. Lay some moist cotton across the top of the glass.

3. Put the dry lima beans on the cotton.

4. Soon the leaves will appear and the roots will grow all the way down into the water. When that happens, plant your lima bean plants in a flowerpot.

Sweet Potatoes

1. Fill a glass three quarters of the way to the top with warm water.

2. Place the fat end of a sweet potato in the glass. Make sure the other end is out of the water.

3. When the roots begin to grow and the leaves start to sprout, plant the sweet potato in a flowerpot.

All Dressed Up!

Karen loves making salad dressing to pour on her very own vegetables. Here are two of her favorite recipes. They taste so, so good!

Farm-Fresh Italian Dressing

You will need:
olive oil
vinegar
lemon juice
dill
garlic
salt
pepper

Here's what you do:
1. Mix together ¼ cup oil with ¼ cup vinegar.
2. Add a splash of lemon juice.
3. Add the dill, garlic, salt, and pepper to taste.
4. Refrigerate.
5. Shake and serve over fresh vegetables.

Really Yummy Russian Dressing

You will need:
ketchup
mayonnaise
pickle relish
salt
pepper

Here's what you do:
1. Mix together ¼ cup ketchup with ¼ cup mayonnaise.
2. Stir in a teaspoon of pickle relish.
3. Add salt and pepper to taste.
4. Refrigerate.
5. Stir well and serve over fresh vegetables.

Never-Bored Board Game Ideas!

You can make board games just like Karen and Tia, the Invention Sisters! Copy the instructions Karen gives you on pages 55 and 56 to make the boards and spinners. Use the spinners to tell you how many spaces to move. Then, instead of playing On the Farm, add your own themes to the games. Here are some ideas for your own board game themes!

Visit to Stoneybrook!

This game is a super salute to Karen's hometown. *Start* is at the Big House. *Finish* is at the Little House. Fill in the spaces on your board with sayings about Karen. Here are a few ideas, and of course, you can add some of your own:

"You were caught using your outdoor voice indoors. Go back one space."

"The Krushers won a softball game! Move ahead two spaces!"

"Stay here and keep an eye on Morbidda Destiny. Lose a turn."

"Nannie takes you for a ride in the Pink Clinker. Spin again."

Silly Stuff Board Game

This game will keep you giggling as you go around the board. To make the game, fill in each square on the board with a silly stunt. When a player lands on a space, he or she has to do the silly stunt written on the square. Keep going until someone lands at the finish space. Here are a few ideas for stunts. Add more of your own:

"Make the silliest face you can."

"Hop on one leg and sing *The Flintstones* theme song."

"Bark like a dog."

"Make believe you are a chicken and walk around the room clucking and flapping your wings."

Super Chutes and Ladders!

To make your own Super Chutes and Ladders game, set up your game board with 50 spaces. Number them as you see in the picture. Draw an equal number of chutes and ladders coming from the spaces. When a player lands on a chute, he or she must sink down to the space where the chute lands. If the player lands on a ladder, he or she climbs up to a higher space. The first player to reach the end wins!

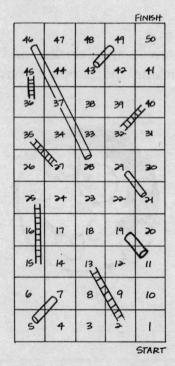

Print Hints!

You can make potato prints just like Karen's!

You will need:
1 large potato cut in half
1 spoon
1 paintbrush
a saucer of tempera paint
construction paper

Here's what you do:
1. Use the spoon to scoop out designs in each of the potato halves. Use the end of the paintbrush to poke holes into your design.
2. Dip your potato design-side down into the paint.
3. Press the potato onto the paper. Carefully lift the potato. Your design will be printed on the paper.
4. Repeat steps 2 and 3 using different colors of paint.

If you want to make a special design, ask a grown-up to help you make these super-deluxe potato prints.
1. Use a knife to carve out designs into the potato half. If you are carving out any words or letters, remember, whatever you carve out will appear-

backwards when you make your print. So write the letters in reverse.

2. Repeat steps 2 and 3 above.

Here are some cool shapes you and a grown-up can make using a knife.

Egg-citing News!

Karen had never seen a real chick hatch before! Did you know that crocodiles, lizards, snakes, and some fish hatch from eggs? The giant dinosaurs hatched from eggs, too!

Fast Facts About Animals!

Amaze your pals with these amazing animal facts!

Did you know that animal mommies keep track of their babies by smell? Every animal baby has his or her own smell, and the mother animal adds to that by licking her babies. The mother's sense of smell is so keen, she can tell her babies from all the others.

Did you know that pigs make real pigs out of themselves? That's right, they'll eat anything that's edible, including acorns, eggs, tree bark, and plant roots. Pigs are smart, too. They can't be herded like other animals, because pigs will only go where they want to go!

Did you know that mother cats have their kittens in dark places? That's to protect the kittens' eyes from the light. Newborn kittens don't open their eyes all the way for eight to ten days. The bright light on their new eyes could hurt them.

Karen's Top Ten Books to Read!

If you're going on a long trip, you'd better load up on fun things to do. For starters, why not take along some of these books? They're Karen's favorites!

1. *Little Toot*, by Hardie Gramatkie
2. *The Witch Next Door*, by Norman Bridwell
3. *Winnie-the-Pooh*, by A. A. Milne
4. *Mrs. Frisby and the Rats of NIMH*, by Robert C. O'Brien
5. *Charlotte's Web*, by E. B. White
6. *Mrs. Piggle-Wiggle*, by Betty MacDonald
7. *Matilda*, by Roald Dahl
8. *Charlie and the Chocolate Factory*, by Roald Dahl
9. *James and the Giant Peach*, by Roald Dahl
10. *The Witches*, by Roald Dahl

Gigundo-Great Games to Play!

These fun games are great for the plane, train, car, or just about anywhere!

Tic-Tac-Toe

This game's an old favorite! All you need is a pencil and some paper.

Here's what you do:
You be X. Your pal will be O. Draw a grid like the one you see in the picture.

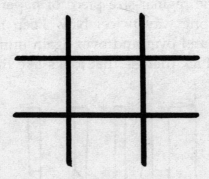

Decide which player will go first. The first player puts his or her mark in a square. Now it is the second player's turn. The first player to get three of his or her symbols in a straight line — up, down, across, or diagonally — is the winner!

Toe-Tac-Tic

For Tic-Tac-Toe with a switch, try this game. The rules are the same as Tic-Tac-Toe, with one change. . . . Any player to get three of his or her symbols in a straight line — up, down, across, or diagonally — loses!

Paper Football Fun!

Here's a way to play football — inside! And the best part is, you don't even need a ball!

Take one regular-size piece of paper. Fold it in half the long way twice. Now keep folding one end over and over and over again until you have a small, thick triangle that looks like this:

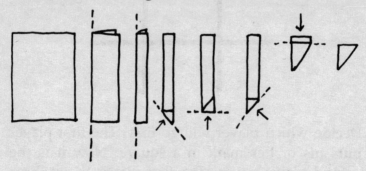

Tuck in the loose end. Now you have a football!

You need two players to play this game. The players sit at opposite ends of the table and take turns shooting the football across the table. The player does this with his or her index finger. No fair sliding the football!

If a player shoots the football to the edge of the table so that part of the football is hanging over the edge, that's a touchdown! If the football falls off the table, it doesn't count. A touchdown is worth six points. The player who has scored the touchdown takes the football back to his or her side of the table and holds it upright, as you see in the picture below. The other player must put his or her index fingers together to form a goalpost at the opposite end of the table. Now the player with the football must use his or her index finger and thumb to kick the football across the table and through the goalpost. If that play succeeds, he or she gets an extra point! Keep playing until one player scores more than 21 points.

You'll love this word game — once you get the *hang* of it!

To play Hangman, divide your friends into two equal teams.

The first team chooses a word. The word should have at least five letters in it. Don't tell the word to the other team. On a piece of paper, the team captain draws one dash for every letter in the word. For example, you would draw eight dashes for AIRPLANE: _ _ _ _ _ _ _ _ .

Now the second team must start to fill in the blanks of the mystery word by guessing letters. If the second team guesses a letter that is in the word, the first team's captain must write the letter in every blank where it appears. For example, *A*: A _ _ _ _ A _ _ . If the second team guesses the wrong letter, the first team's captain draws the first part of the hanging man.

Throughout the game, the first team adds a new part of the hanging man's body each time a wrong letter is guessed. If the hanging man is completed before the second team guesses the mystery word, they lose the game. If the team guesses the word before the hanging man is completed, they win the game. This is what the hanging man should look like:

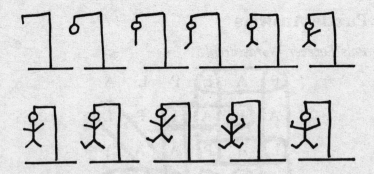

Ghost!

Ghost is one game that will keep you spellbound! To play, three or more players sit in a row. The first player begins by saying any letter of the alphabet. The next player adds a letter. Each player must add a letter, but no one can complete a word (two-letter words don't count). The player who spells a word loses that round and earns a letter G. Each time a player loses a round, he or she adds another letter to the word *ghost*. When a player has lost five rounds, he or she is out. The last player left in the game wins.

Puzzle Answers

Pals Forever Wordsearch!

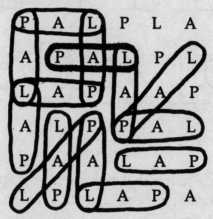

Karen Two-Two's Count by Twos Puzzle

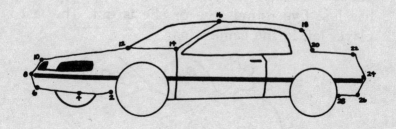

Karen's Crossword Puzzle

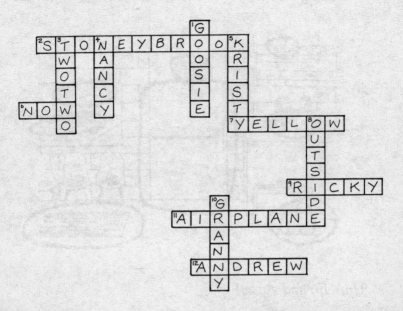

Spellbound

1. CAN
2. CAT
3. COT
4. NOT
5. TAN
6. TIN
7. VAT
8. AT
9. IN
10. ON

Something's Different

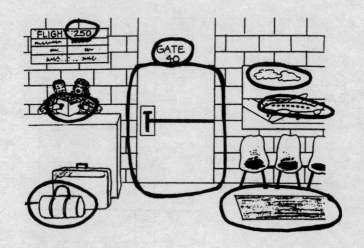

Up, Up, and Away!

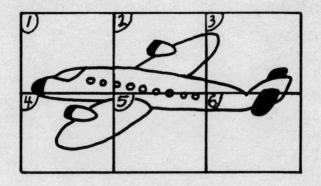

Life on a Farm

Find Your Plane Airport Maze

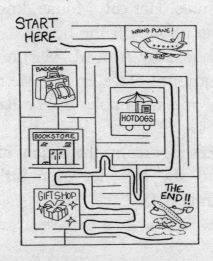

About the Author

ANN M. MARTIN lives in New York City and loves animals. Her cat, Mouse, knows how to take the phone off the hook.

Other books by Ann M. Martin that you might enjoy are *Stage Fright, Me and Katie (the Pest)*, and the books in *The Baby-sitters Club* series.

Ann likes ice cream, the beach, and *I Love Lucy*. And she has her own little sister, whose name is Jane.

LITTLE 🍎 APPLE®

BABYSITTERS
Little Sister®
by Ann M. Martin, author of The Baby-sitters Club ®

☐ MQ44300-3	#1	Karen's Witch	$2.75
☐ MQ44259-7	#2	Karen's Roller Skates	$2.75
☐ MQ44299-7	#3	Karen's Worst Day	$2.75
☐ MQ44264-3	#4	Karen's Kittycat Club	$2.75
☐ MQ44258-9	#5	Karen's School Picture	$2.75
☐ MQ43651-1	#10	Karen's Grandmothers	$2.75
☐ MQ43650-3	#11	Karen's Prize	$2.75
☐ MQ43649-X	#12	Karen's Ghost	$2.75
☐ MQ43648-1	#13	Karen's Surprise	$2.75
☐ MQ43646-5	#14	Karen's New Year	$2.75
☐ MQ43645-7	#15	Karen's In Love	$2.75
☐ MQ43644-9	#16	Karen's Goldfish	$2.75
☐ MQ43643-0	#17	Karen's Brothers	$2.75
☐ MQ43642-2	#18	Karen's Home-Run	$2.75
☐ MQ43641-4	#19	Karen's Good-Bye	$2.95
☐ MQ44823-4	#20	Karen's Carnival	$2.75
☐ MQ44824-2	#21	Karen's New Teacher	$2.95
☐ MQ44833-1	#22	Karen's Little Witch	$2.95
☐ MQ44832-3	#23	Karen's Doll	$2.95
☐ MQ44859-5	#24	Karen's School Trip	$2.75
☐ MQ44831-5	#25	Karen's Pen Pal	$2.75
☐ MQ44830-7	#26	Karen's Ducklings	$2.75
☐ MQ44829-3	#27	Karen's Big Joke	$2.75
☐ MQ44828-5	#28	Karen's Tea Party	$2.75
☐ MQ44825-0	#29	Karen's Cartwheel	$2.75
☐ MQ45645-8	#30	Karen's Kittens	$2.75
☐ MQ45646-6	#31	Karen's Bully	$2.95
☐ MQ45647-4	#32	Karen's Pumpkin Patch	$2.95
☐ MQ45648-2	#33	Karen's Secret	$2.95
☐ MQ45650-4	#34	Karen's Snow Day	$2.95
☐ MQ45652-0	#35	Karen's Doll Hosital	$2.95